A Movie Star

Random House 🏠 New York

Published in the United States by Random House Children's Books,
a division of Random House, Inc., 1745 Broadway, New York, NY 10019,
and in Canada by Random House of Canada Limited, Toronto.
No part of this book may be reproduced or copied in any form without permission from the copyright owner.
Random House and the colophon are registered trademarks of Random House, Inc.
The stories contained in this work were orginally published separately in slightly different form by Golden Books under
the following titles: *A Dream Come True!* in 2003, *Rodeo Cowgirl!* in 2003, and *Super Spy* in 2005.
Library of Congress Control Number: 2009939459   ISBN: 978-0-375-86089-8
www.randomhouse.com/kids   MANUFACTURED IN SINGAPORE   10 9 8 7 6 5 4 3 2 1

Contents

6

*B*arbie stars in a show by her community theater group, and a famous movie director notices her wonderful performance.

"What a talent!" says the director, Mr. Barrett. "Barbie's perfect for my next film."

After the play, Mr. Barrett introduces himself to Barbie. "How would you like to audition for my new movie, *The Secret*?"

"Would I ever!" says Barbie as her eyes light up. She has always wanted to be in the movies.

9

Barbie goes to the movie studio the next day. She reads lines from *The Secret* for Mr. Barrett.

"The jewels are hidden," says Barbie, reading from the script. "And you'll never find them."

Mr. Barrett claps. "Bravo!" he says. "You've got the part of the young countess in my new movie. The shoot starts next month."

"Wow!" cries Barbie. "The movies! This is a dream come true!"

MAKE-UP

On the first day of the shoot, Barbie meets the cast and crew. Mr. Barrett is busy giving instructions to some of the actors on the set.

STAGE #1

"Places, everyone!" says Mr. Barrett.
The actors take their positions.
"Action!" he cries.

13

A production assistant takes Barbie to Costume Design.
"Look at all these beautiful clothes!" says Barbie.
Then Barbie tries on her countess outfit.

After her costume fitting, Barbie goes to Hair and Makeup.
When she's all ready, the stylist turns Barbie toward the mirror.
"Wow!" says Barbie. "I feel like royalty."

On the movie set, Barbie meets the leading lady, Nikki O'Neil. Barbie watches Nikki get ready for one of the most dramatic scenes in the movie. Nikki reads the letter in her hand, and then she starts to cry.

After the scene is over, everyone applauds.

"That was terrific," says Barbie. "Nikki's a great actress."

There is a lot of activity on the set. The gaffer makes sure the lighting is perfect. Then the cinematographer adjusts his camera right before he rolls the film.

STAGE A

"Wow," says Barbie. "A lot of people sure are needed to make a movie happen."

Now it's time to film Barbie's scene.
"Roll 'em!" shouts Mr. Barrett.
"The jewels are hidden," says Barbie.
"And you'll never find them."

Mr. Barrett tells Barbie to act angry and storm out of the room. After a few takes, the scene is perfect. Mr. Barrett is pleased with Barbie's performance. "Great job, Barbie!" he says through his megaphone.

After Mr. Barrett finishes making *The Secret*, he throws a cast party. Everyone has a great time.

When *The Secret* hits movie theaters, the critics love it, and Nikki O'Neil is nominated for a Shining Star Award.

The SECRET

The Times

NOMINATED
— FOR —
SHINING STAR AWARD

The Secr
★★★

Mr. Barrett has an extra ticket to the Shining Star Awards, and he sends it to Barbie.

Barbie wears her new pink satin gown.

"This is so exciting," Barbie says. The cameras flash as she walks down the red carpet to the awards show.

At the ceremony, the host announces the winner for best actress. He tears open the envelope.
"And the winner is . . .

. . . Nikki O'Neil!"

The orchestra plays music from *The Secret* as Nikki walks onto the stage. She holds her golden trophy high.

"Wow," says Barbie. "Nikki's wonderful. I've learned so much from her and from all of you."

"You *have* learned a lot, Barbie," says Mr. Barrett.

"Acting is hard work, and so much fun!" says Barbie. "I learned a lot about how a movie is made. I know I can be an actress, too! I can't wait to audition for a lead role in *Rodeo Cowgirl!*"

"Hi!" says Barbie. "Welcome to the set of my newest movie, *Rodeo Cowgirl*. I'm a little nervous because this is the first film where I have the starring role.

30

"But I'm also very excited. I play a cowgirl named Samantha Jacobs. And I get to wear all these great Western costumes. Cool, huh?"

"Places, everyone!" calls the director.

"Well, I'd better get ready," says Barbie. "See you after the shoot!"

In the Wild West, a daring and beautiful wrangler rides the new frontier.
"Ride 'em, cowgirl!" cry the cowboys.

"Yeehaw!" shouts Samantha.

Samantha can do anything a cowboy can do. She saddles her horse, Bandit, and ropes cattle with a lariat. "Yippee-i-ay!" Samantha cries as she twirls a rope over her head.

Samantha also loves to spend time riding her horse. She has just learned a new trick—riding sidesaddle.

Samantha's mother and father own a big farm. This year there hasn't been enough rain. The crops did not grow.

One morning Samantha hears her parents talking to a man from the local bank. The banker says that Samantha's family will lose their farm if they don't pay their bills.

"Just give us a few months and we'll have enough money," says Samantha's father.

"Sorry," says the banker. "We can't wait that long. You have until the end of the week to pay us."

41

"I've got to help Mom and Dad!" says Samantha. "Maybe I can find work in town to earn enough money to save the farm!"

Samantha gets dressed.

Then she saddles Bandit and races downtown.

At the general store, Samantha scans the town bulletin board.

"Good morning, Samantha," says the sheriff. "What brings you to town so early?"

ANNUAL RODEO U Sign Up

WANTED One Lovely Dance Partner

44

"Our farm is in trouble," says Samantha. "I'm looking for work so I can save it."

"Why don't you enter the rodeo?" suggests the sheriff. "First prize is five hundred dollars."

"That's a great idea," says Samantha.

The rodeo is in five days! Samantha practices her cowgirl skills.

And she gets Bandit ready for the big show.

On the day of the rodeo, crowds fill the stands.

Samantha is in almost every event. She rides a bucking bronco.

"Wahoo!" yells Samantha.

She even ropes a calf on her first try.
"Yeehaw!" she shouts.

At the end of the day, the announcer says, "First prize goes to Miss Samantha Jacobs!"

Samantha proudly hands the trophy full of prize money to her parents.

"Our farm is saved!" they cry.

That night Samantha's family and friends
throw a special celebration in her honor.
Everyone has a great time, and Samantha
do-si-dos all night long.

51

"Cut!" yells the director. "That's a wrap!"
"Whew!" says Barbie. "I had a lot of fun making my first Wild West movie. I hope you liked it. See you soon!"

Barbie i can be...

"Hi there!" says Barbie. "I'm in France to shoot my new movie, *Super Spy*. In this film, I play Crystal Peters, a secret agent on a dangerous mission."

"Places!" shouts the director.
"Well, I'd better get going," says Barbie.
"Hope you enjoy the show!"

55

On a beautiful beach in France, secret agent Crystal Peters gets a call on her wrist communicator from Super Spy headquarters.

"Crystal," says Chief Ian Jones, "the Pink Star diamond has been stolen! It needs to be returned to the Museum of Rare Gems right away."

"Do we have any suspects, Ian?" Crystal asks.

"We believe Countess Devinshark has the diamond," replies Ian.

"You can depend on me," says Crystal. "The Pink Star will be in the right hands in no time."

57

Before Crystal starts her mission, she goes to the secret equipment facility.

"You've outdone yourself, Jenkins!" says Crystal to the equipment specialist. "All these gadgets are cool—and stylish!"

Crystal jumps on her motorcycle and follows the long, winding road to Countess Devinshark's mansion.

"Here we go!" she says, hopping off her motorcycle.

Taking her bag loaded with gear, Crystal heads for the castle.

In her special hover boots, Crystal sprints across the castle moat. Then she checks out the mansion—all the entrances are blocked by guards.

Suddenly, Crystal spots a secret way in.

"The air-conditioning shaft!" she exclaims.
Prying off the grate, Crystal crawls inside and slides
down the shaft. Then she uses her mini-computer to locate
the Pink Star diamond.

"Oh, no!" groans Crystal as she takes a peek into the heavily secured room.

Pink laser beams crisscross the room—one false move and she will trigger the alarm system.

"I know . . . ," Crystal says. She pulls two special cosmetic mirrors from her leather bag and deactivates the laser beams. "No problem!"

Crystal carefully lowers herself into the room. The Pink
Star shimmers and sparkles in front of her.
    "Wow!" says Crystal. "Now, that's what I call one big rock!"
    She quickly disarms the laser beam alarms and grabs the
diamond. Then she runs out of the room . . .

. . . right into Countess Devinshark and her guards!
"Where do you think you're going with *my*
diamond?" demands Countess Devinshark as she
snatches the jewel from Crystal.

"It belongs to the Museum of Rare Gems!" Crystal says. Using her karate skills, Crystal breaks free from the guards—and kicks the diamond right out of the countess's hand!

"Time to rock 'n' roll out of here!" says Crystal as she catches the diamond and sprints across the moat.
"After her!" Countess Devinshark yells to her men.

Crystal jumps on her motorcycle and speeds off. But Countess Devinshark and her guards quickly follow her in their car.

"When will these criminals learn?" Crystal asks herself. She pushes a button and activates a smoke screen. The countess and her men are stopped in their tracks!

"Mission accomplished," Crystal says.

At the Museum of Rare Gems, Crystal shimmers in a sparkly pink gown.

"Well done, Crystal!" says Ian. "I knew you'd recover the Pink Star diamond."

"You know what they say," Crystal jokes. "Diamonds are a girl's best friend!"

"Cut!" calls the director. "Fantastic job, Barbie."
"I had a blast!" says Barbie. "I hope you liked
Super Spy! See you all at my next movie!"